Pig Is
Big on
Books

Pig Is Big
on Books

DOUGLAS FLORIAN

I Like to Read®

HOLIDAY HOUSE • NEW YORK

In memory of Diane Florian

I LIKE TO READ is a registered trademark of Holiday House, Inc.

Copyright © 2015 by Douglas Florian
All Rights Reserved
HOLIDAY HOUSE is registered in the U.S. Patent and Trademark Office.
Printed and Bound in July 2019 at Tien Wah Press, Johor Bahru, Johor, Malaysia.
The artwork was created with gouache watercolor, colored pencil and
collage on primed paper bag.
www.holidayhouse.com
First Edition
5 7 9 10 8 6 4

Library of Congress Cataloging-in-Publication Data
Florian, Douglas, author, illustrator.
Pig is big on books / Douglas Florian. — First edition.
pages cm. — (I like to read)
Summary: Pig loves books, both big and small, and
reads them at school, at home, and on the bus.
ISBN 978-0-8234-3393-3 (hardcover)
[1. Books and reading—Fiction. 2. Pigs—Fiction.] I. Title.
PZ7.F6645Pi 2015
[E]—dc23
2014032162

ISBN 978-0-8234-3424-4 (paperback)

Pig is big on books.

Pig likes to read.

Pig reads big books.

Pig is glad.

Pig reads small books.

Pig reads at home.

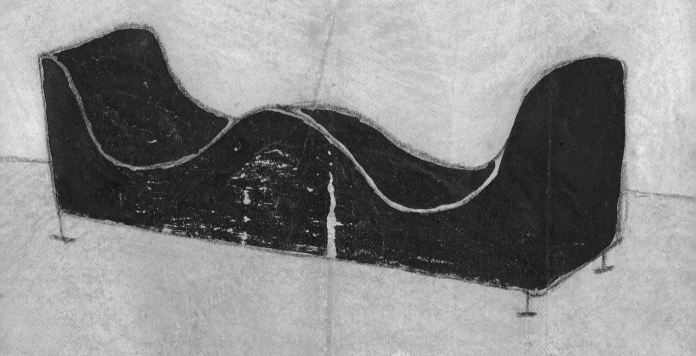

Pig reads at school.

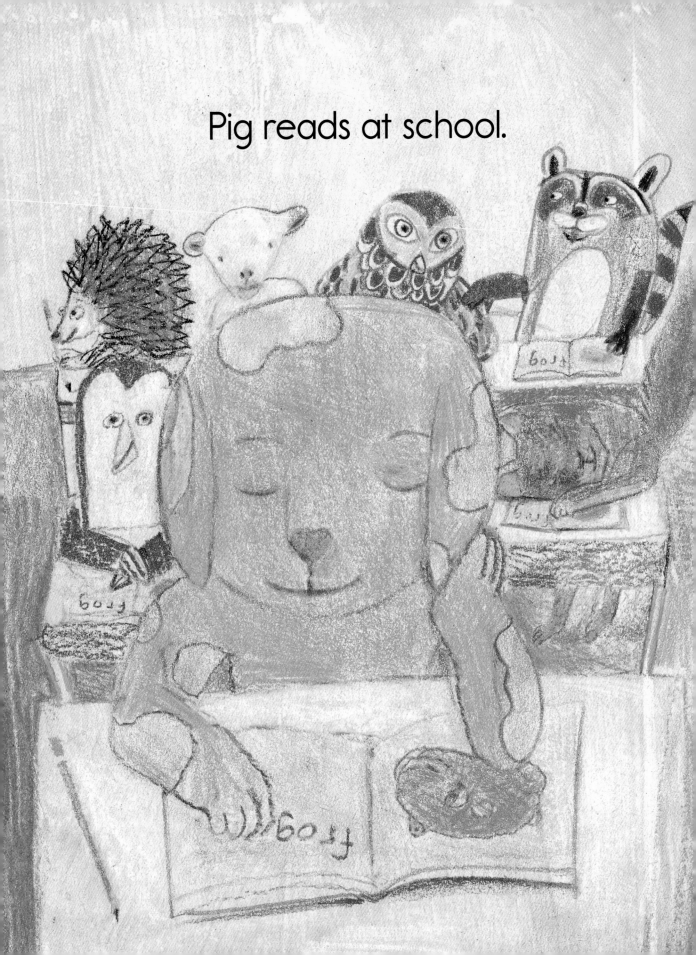

Pig reads on the bus.

Pig reads with Cat.

And Pig reads with his mom.

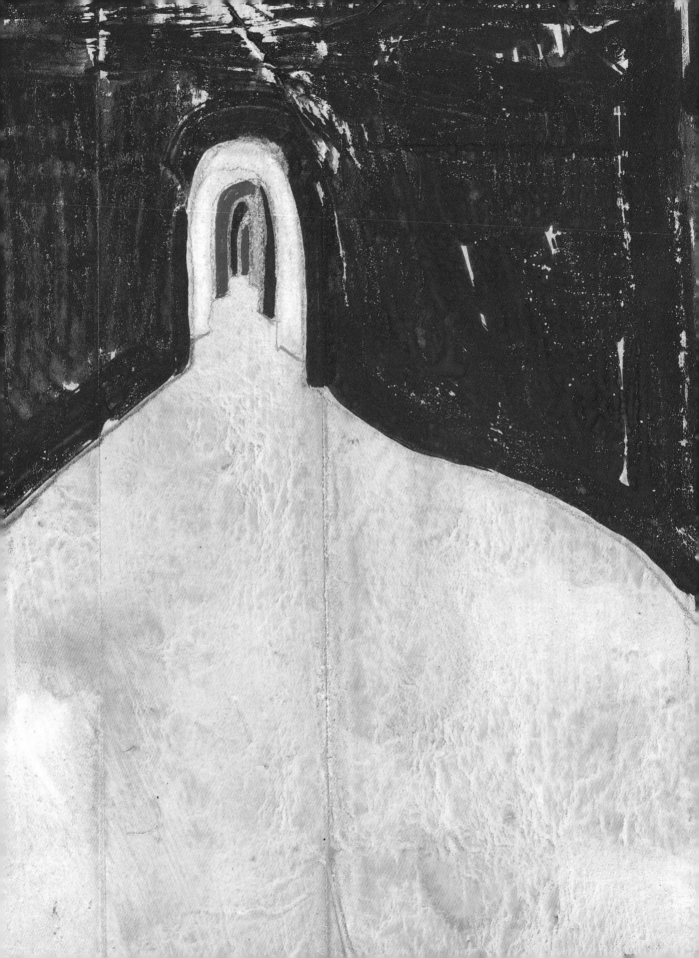

One day Pig had no books.

Pig looked and looked.

He did not find even one book.

So Pig wrote a book.

Pig is big on books.

Pig wrote **this** book.

Pig reads small books.

Pig reads at school.

Pig reads with Cat.

Pig reads big books.

You will like these too!

Come Back, Ben by Ann Hassett and John Hassett
A *Kirkus Reviews* Best Book

Dinosaurs Don't, Dinosaurs Do by Steve Björkman
A Notable Social Studies Trade Book for Young People
An IRA/CBC Children's Choice

Fish Had a Wish by Michael Garland
A *Kirkus Reviews* Best Book
A Top 25 Children's Books list book

The Fly Flew In by David Catrow
An IRA/CBC Children's Choice
Maryland Blue Crab Young Reader Award Winner

Look! by Ted Lewin
The Correll Book Award for Excellence
in Early Childhood Informational Text

Me Too! by Valeri Gorbachev
A Bank Street Best Book of the Year

Mice on Ice by Rebecca Emberley and Ed Emberley
A Bank Street Best Children's Book of the Year
An IRA/CBC Children's Choice

Pig Has a Plan by Ethan Long
An IRA/CBC Children's Choice

See Me Dig by Paul Meisel
A *Kirkus Reviews* Best Book

See Me Run by Paul Meisel
A Theodor Seuss Geisel Award Honor Book
An ALA Notable Children's Book

You Can Do It! by Betsy Lewin
A Bank Street Best Children's Book of the Year,
Outstanding Merit

See more I Like to Read® books.
Go to www.holidayhouse.com/I-Like-to-Read/

Some More I Like to Read® Books
in Paperback

Animals Work by Ted Lewin

Bad Dog by David McPhail

Can You See Me? by Ted Lewin

Cat Got a Lot by Steve Henry

The Fly Flew In by David Catrow

Happy Cat by Steve Henry

I Have a Garden by Bob Barner

Little Ducks Go by Emily Arnold McCully

Me Too! by Valeri Gorbachev

Mice on Ice by Rebecca Emberley and Ed Emberley

Pig Has a Plan by Ethan Long

Pig Is Big on Books by Douglas Florian

What Am I? Where Am I? by Ted Lewin

You Can Do It! by Betsy Lewin

Visit http://www.holidayhouse.com/I-Like-to-Read/ for more about I Like to Read® books, including flash cards, reproducibles and the complete list of titles.